This
MOUSE ∞ WORKS
Classics Collection Storybook

belongs to

Natalie Sax
Natalie Sasha

CLASSIC STORYBOOK

WALT DISNEY PICTURES PRESENTS "MULAN"
MUSIC BY MATTHEW WILDER LYRICS BY DAVID ZIPPEL ORIGINAL SCORE BY JERRY GOLDSMITH
PRODUCED BY PAM COATS DIRECTED BY BARRY COOK AND TONY BANCROFT
DISTRIBUTED BY BUENA VISTA PICTURES DISTRIBUTION, INC. © DISNEY ENTERPRISES, INC.

MOUSE WORKS

Find us at **www.disneybooks.com** *for more Mouse Works fun!*

© 1998 Disney Enterprises, Inc.
Adapted by Lisa Ann Marsoli
Illustrated by Judith Holmes Clarke, Brent Ford, Denise Shimabukuro,
Scott Tilley, Lori Tyminski, and Atelier Philippe Harchy
Printed in the United States of America
ISBN: 1-57082-864-4
1 3 5 7 9 10 8 6 4 2

Thousands of years ago, a wise emperor built a wall
to keep invaders out of China. As time passed, each
new emperor added to the wall until it stretched for
many miles, guarding the people like a great dragon.
But one day a ferocious Hun leader named Shan-Yu
breached the Great Wall, and led his fierce soldiers
into China.

As soon as General Li, the commander of the Imperial Army, delivered the news of the Huns' invasion, the Emperor ordered his aide, Chi Fu, to deliver conscription notices throughout all the provinces.

"A single grain of rice can tip the scale," the Emperor wisely noted. "One man may be the difference between victory and defeat."

Far from the Imperial Palace, a young woman named Mulan was busily writing notes on her arm. Today was the day for her meeting with the Matchmaker, and she wanted to be prepared. If she performed well, she would bring honor to her family by making a good match in marriage.

Mulan worked quickly because she was already late. She rewarded her dog, Little Brother, with a bone for helping her with her chores. Then she brought tea to her beloved father, Fa Zhou.

Fa Zhou was at the family temple praying to the Ancestors to guide his daughter that day. When he saw Mulan, he urged her to be on her way.

9

In the nearby village, Mulan's mother, Fa Li, watched in horror as her mother-in-law closed her eyes and crossed the busy street. Grandmother Fa was testing a new lucky cricket. Speeding carts and carriages swerved all around her, but Grandmother Fa and "Cri-Kee" arrived safely on the other side of the street.

"Yep," proclaimed Grandmother Fa, "this cricket's a lucky one!"

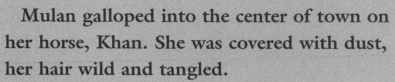

Mulan galloped into the center of town on
her horse, Khan. She was covered with dust,
her hair wild and tangled.

"I'm here!" she announced proudly when she
saw her mother.

Fa Li rushed Mulan off to the skillful artists who soon transformed her into a delicate Chinese maiden.

As a finishing touch, Fa Li gave Mulan a hair comb that had been in the family for many generations. Then Grandmother Fa gave Mulan an apple for serenity, a jade necklace for beauty, and Cri-Kee for good luck.

Unfortunately, everything seemed to go wrong when Mulan met with the Matchmaker. First the ink from Mulan's arm smeared on the Matchmaker's face. Then Cri-Kee took a swim in the Matchmaker's tea. As Mulan tried to grab the cup, hot tea spilled everywhere. This caused the Matchmaker to fall onto a lighted stove, where her clothes caught fire!

17

The Matchmaker ran outside screaming. Thinking quickly, Mulan drenched the woman with tea to put out the fire.

"You will never bring your family honor!" the irate Matchmaker shouted at Mulan.

Mulan could scarcely hold her head up
as she led Khan home. She had done the
unthinkable: She had disgraced her family.
Looking at her image in the temple beis,
Mulan knew that she would never truly
be the delicate Chinese maiden she saw
looking back at her.

Sadly Mulan went to sit under a tree in the garden. Her father quietly joined her and gestured up to a branch.

"This blossom's late," Fa Zhou said. "But I'll bet that when it blooms, it will be the most beautiful of all."

Mulan managed to smile, but the quiet moment was cut short by the sound of a drum and approaching horses.

"The Huns have invaded China!" Chi Fu announced. "One man from every family must serve in the Imperial Army!"

When the Fa family was called, Mulan rushed forward and begged Chi Fu not to take her father, who had already served the Emperor bravely. Chi Fu was furious that a woman would speak to him directly. Mulan hung her head. She had shamed her family again.

Later Fa Zhou took his sword from his armor cabinet. Unaware that Mulan was watching, he started to practice some fighting moves.

Suddenly a pain from an old wound shot through his leg, and he crumpled to the floor. In that instant, Mulan knew that her father would never survive another journey into battle.

That evening Mulan made her decision. After she
said a prayer to her Ancestors, she went to the main
house and quietly took her father's conscription
notice from his table, replacing it with the hair comb
her mother had given her.

Swiftly, Mulan cut her long black hair with her
father's sword. Then she donned his armor and went
out to the stables to get Khan.

As she headed out into the darkness, Mulan's only thought was to save her father's life.

A short while later, Grandmother Fa awakened Mulan's parents. But it was too late to stop their beloved Mulan. Grandmother Fa desperately prayed to the family Ancestors, asking them to keep Mulan safe. They all knew that if Mulan were caught, she would be killed.

In the Fa family temple, the spirits of the Ancestors gathered. A small dragon incense burner named Mushu had once been a Guardian and wanted to regain his position by saving Mulan. But when he tried to blow an impressive flame, his little sputter merely met with laughter. Instead of being sent to bring Mulan home, Mushu was told to wake up the Great Stone Dragon to carry out the important task.

Mushu went outside to try to rouse the dragon. He hit it with his gong. Suddenly, the dragon crumbled beneath him! Not wanting the Ancestors to know what had happened, Mushu decided to impersonate the dragon, holding its head high enough for the Ancestors to see.

Moments later, when Cri-Kee appeared, Mushu agreed to go after Mulan. He thought that if he made Mulan a hero, he would get back his job as Guardian.

Early the next morning, Mushu and Cri-Kee found Mulan outside the army camp. Mushu lit a fire and cast his impressive-looking shadow against a rock. Then, in his mightiest voice, he roared that he had been sent by Mulan's Ancestors to guide her. When Mulan finally saw Mushu up close, she thought he looked more like a lizard than an all-powerful Guardian. But she also knew she needed all the help she could get.

Later, when Mulan arrived at the army camp, Mushu hid in her collar and whispered advice on how to blend in with the men. Mulan tried his suggestions on the first three recruits she met, Yao, Ling, and Chien-Po.

But Mushu's advice was not very good. Mulan soon found herself a witness to a free-for-all—and she had started it!

Meanwhile, in an officer's tent, Chi Fu was meeting with General Li and the general's son, Shang. The general surprised both men by promoting Shang to the rank of captain.

Before leaving to lead his troops to the Tung-Shao Pass, General Li put Chi Fu in charge of reporting on Shang's progress in training the recruits.

After his father had gone, Shang went to the center of camp, where he discovered all his recruits engaged in a huge brawl. The others wasted no time in pointing out Mulan as the source of the trouble.

"What is your name?" Shang asked Mulan.

"My name? It's—uh—Ping!" she replied. Handing Shang her conscription notice, Mulan knew she was not off to a good start.

The next morning, the recruits began their training. Their first exercise was to retrieve an arrow that Shang had shot to the top of a tall pole. As part of the lesson, they were required to wear two large bronze disks—one tied to each wrist.

"One represents discipline, the other strength," Shang said of the disks. "You need both to reach the arrow."

Yao, Ling, Chien-Po, and Mulan all failed to reach the arrow. For another exercise, Shang gave everyone a long pole to wield as a weapon. Mulan tried the best she could, but the other recruits kept tripping her up. She performed miserably.

Shang continued drilling the recruits throughout the following weeks, attempting to teach strength and discipline. But it was clear to him that he was not getting through to them—especially Mulan. The arrow in the pole proved his point. Finally, one day when he saw Mulan collapse on the ground, he ordered her to go home.

48

As she turned to go, Mulan spied the arrow still embedded in the
top of the pole. Determined to try one last time, she put the weights
on her wrists and began to climb. As before, she fell. Then, after
studying the weights, she had an idea. She looped them together and
used them as a brace to hoist herself to the top.

Her fellow recruits cheered. Even Shang had to admire her.

Deep in the countryside, Shan-Yu's falcon delivered a child's doll to his master. Shan-Yu showed his men how to decipher its significance. They discovered the doll had come from the Tung-Shao Pass—and that General Li's army was waiting there for them.

"Come," Shan-Yu told his men with a sinister sneer. "The little girl must be missing her doll. We should return it to her."

Mulan went to a lake near the camp to bathe. Soon Ling, Yao, and Chien-Po joined her! They apologized for how they had acted earlier and tried to get their friend "Ping" to engage in some good-natured horseplay. Luckily Mulan was saved from embarrassment when Mushu bit Ling. The diversion gave Mulan time to escape and get back into her clothes.

Mushu knew that in order to make Mulan a hero, he had to get her into battle. So after Mulan had returned to her tent, Mushu got Cri-Kee to help him compose a letter from General Li, ordering that Shang and his men meet him at the Tung-Shao Pass.

Heeding the letter's message, Shang led his troops into the mountains. There they came upon a village that had been burned by the Huns. Chien-Po found General Li's helmet in the destruction of the battlefield.

Silently, Shang plunged his sword into the snow, placing his father's helmet on top of it. At the base of the tribute, Mulan placed a child's doll she had found among the wreckage.

"We're the Emperor's only hope," Shang said to his troops. "Move out!"

Shang's troops marched silently through the Tung-Shao Pass. Suddenly a rocket from the munitions wagon exploded. It signaled the position of Shang's troops to the waiting Huns. Instantly, thousands of flaming arrows showered down from the mountains.

Mulan untied Khan just before the munitions wagon exploded. Mushu and Cri-Kee were barely thrown to safety in the blast.

Mulan raced to join the other soldiers. Shang's troops fired their cannons. For a moment, the Huns disappeared. Then hundreds of the enemy soldiers began to pour over the mountaintop. Shang's troops were hopelessly outnumbered. Bravely, Shang ordered Yao to point the last cannon at Shan-Yu.

Mulan got an idea. She grabbed Yao's cannon and ran toward the Huns. When she had almost reached Shan-Yu, Mulan lit her cannon.

It flew through the air, and landed in the mountain, causing a massive avalanche which cascaded down upon the Huns.

Shan-Yu was furious. He slashed at Mulan, seeking revenge on the soldier responsible for destroying his army.

As the avalanche gained speed, Shan-Yu turned to ride to safety but was soon buried in snow.

Yao, Ling, and Chien-Po took shelter with some other soldiers, while Mushu escaped by riding a shield like a bobsled.

Khan raced toward Mulan. She jumped onto his back, then reached to pull Shang up behind her just before a wall of snow threw them over a cliff.

From above, Yao, Ling, and some other soldiers worked desperately to help. But it wasn't until Chien-Po picked up the group of soldiers that they were able to pull their comrades to safety.

When Shang recovered, he looked at Mulan. "I owe you my life. From now on, you have my trust."

Mulan suddenly grabbed her side, wincing in pain. After tending to Mulan's wound, the medic revealed the shocking news: "Ping" was really a woman!

Chi Fu demanded that Shang kill Mulan, as was required by the law. Despite feeling hurt and betrayed by Mulan's deception, Shang decided to spare her life. Then he ordered the troops to move out without her.

Mulan sat with Khan, Mushu, and Cri-Kee next to a small fire. "I thought I came here to save my father," she said miserably, "but maybe what I really wanted was to prove I could do things right."

"The Ancestors never even sent me. You risked your life to help people you love," Mushu said to comfort her. "I risked your life to help myself."

Just then a howl sounded in the chasm. Shan-Yu was alive.

Shan-Yu and five of the elite Huns were heading toward the Imperial City. Mulan knew she had to do something. She caught up with Shang just as he and his troops were approaching the Imperial Palace to present Shan-Yu's sword to the Emperor. But Shang still felt betrayed by Mulan and did not believe her.

Shang walked up the steps of the Imperial Palace and bowed to present Shan-Yu's sword to the Emperor.

Suddenly Shan-Yu's falcon swooped down, grabbed the sword, and delivered it to Shan-Yu who was waiting on the rooftop of the Palace. As the crowd watched in horror, a group of Huns slashed their way out of a paper dragon. Moving swiftly, the Huns dragged the Emperor into the Palace and bolted the door.

Nearby Mulan witnessed the commotion and devised a plan. Quickly she helped Yao, Chien-Po, and Ling disguise themselves as women. Then she led them to the side of the Palace, where they wrapped the sashes from their dresses around some pillars. Skillfully, they began to climb—just as they had learned at training camp.

Shang joined them. He had decided to trust Mulan.

Once inside the Imperial Palace, Mulan, Ling, Yao, and Chien-Po knocked out the Hun guards. Then Shang burst onto the balcony where the Emperor was being held and confronted Shan-Yu.

While Shang distracted the evil Hun leader, Chien-Po ran to the Emperor and carried him to the edge of the tower where they slid down a makeshift line. Ling and Yao followed. Quickly Mulan cut the line, so that Shan-Yu would not be able to chase them.

Furious that the Emperor had escaped, Shan-Yu charged toward Shang with his sword drawn.

"You took away my victory," Shan-Yu snarled at Shang.

"No," said Mulan. "I did." Then she pulled back her hair so Shan-Yu would recognize her.

"The soldier from the mountains!" he said, filled with rage.

Shan-Yu raced after Mulan—exactly as she wanted. She led him to the roof where she turned to face him. Then she grabbed his sword and pinned his cloak to the roof. Moments later Mushu arrived with a rocket strapped to his back. When Cri-Kee lit the rocket's fuse, Mushu jumped to safety. The well-aimed rocket knocked Shan-Yu all the way to the fireworks tower.

The force of the huge explosion catapulted Mushu and Cri-Kee through the air. Mulan was thrown against Shang.

An entire wing of the Imperial Palace was in flames. Mulan and Shang turned and stared in awe as fireworks lit up the sky. Soon Yao, Ling, and Chien-Po joined them.

Then the Emperor and Chi Fu approached.

"I have heard a great deal about you, Fa Mulan," the Emperor said sternly. "You stole your father's armor, impersonated a soldier, dishonored the Chinese army, destroyed my palace, and...you have saved us all."

Then the Emperor did something amazing. He bowed to Mulan. Stunned, everyone in the plaza followed the Emperor's example.

The Emperor gave Mulan his pendant, as well as Shan-Yu's sword.
Then Shang bid her an awkward good-bye.

"The flower that blooms in adversity is the most rare and beautiful
of all," the Emperor said to Shang as Mulan rode away. Shang looked
puzzled. "You don't meet a girl like that every dynasty," the Emperor
said pointedly.

At home, Mulan handed her father the Emperor's gifts.

"The greatest gift and honor is having you for a daughter," Fa Zhou said, embracing her. "I've missed you so."

Fa Li and Grandmother Fa watched from a distance.

"Excuse me," said a voice behind them. "Does Fa Mulan live here?" It was Shang. The two women directed him toward Mulan.

To the delight of her entire family, Mulan
invited Shang to stay for dinner.

Meanwhile, in the family temple, the First
Ancestor agreed that Mushu had succeeded in
his mission, and the little dragon was
reinstated as a Family Guardian.

"Call out for eggrolls!" Mushu cried. It was
time to celebrate.

Disney's Classic Storybook COLLECTION™

Relive the movies one book at a time.

ALADDIN
ALICE IN WONDERLAND
THE ARISTOCATS
BAMBI
BEAUTY AND THE BEAST

THE BLACK CAULDRON
CINDERELLA
DUMBO
THE FOX AND THE HOUND
THE GREAT MOUSE DETECTIVE

HERCULES
THE HUNCHBACK OF NOTRE DAME
THE JUNGLE BOOK
LADY AND THE TRAMP
THE LION KING

THE LITTLE MERMAID
MICKEY'S CHRISTMAS CAROL
OLIVER & COMPANY
ONE HUNDRED AND ONE DALMATIA
PETER PAN

PINOCCHIO
POCAHONTAS
THE RESCUERS
THE RESCUERS DOWN UNDER
ROBIN HOOD

SLEEPING BEAUTY
SNOW WHITE AND THE SEVEN DW
THE SWORD IN THE STONE
TOY STORY
WINNIE THE POOH

For you... from MOUSE WORKS

A special invitation to have even more fun—
Free!

Send for a FREE ISSUE of FamilyFun Magazine! It's chock full of fun activities the whole family will love!

★ Easy after-school and rainy-day activities. Like how to create a cloud – or make tin-can stilts!

★ Great crafts & hobbies with step-by-step instructions. Like how to splatter a T-shirt or make thrilling, chilling Halloween costumes!

★ Fun party plans, dynamite decorations, and great games. Like how to dance the hula in a paper grass skirt and make a lei out of pasta!

★ Recipes kids love to make – and eat! Imagine carrot "coins", broccoli "trees", and baked potatoes "a la Mode."

★ And everything else fun from family computing to family traveling to Family Olympics. Imagine tie-dying socks – or making "duck feet" to have a Duck Foot Relay Race!

SPECIAL JOKES & GAMES FOR KIDS

FamilyFun
Halloween Party!
Slimy Games, Zany Food & Other Wicked Fun
Make-your-own Costumes

"What's for Dinner?"
12 Award-winners Kids Eat Up

Teaching Kids About Money
An Age-by-age Activity Guide

Dude Ranch Roundup

The Joy of Autumn
Leaf Games, and a Friendl...

You always know what you'll find in FamilyFun – 100% activities and 100% fun! And it's free with this special invitation!

Just send in the FREE ISSUE Certificate today!

FamilyFun
Free Issue Certificate

Yes! Send my family the next issue of FamilyFun – FREE! If we like it, we'll get a full year (10 big issues in all, including my free issue and TWO SPECIAL ISSUES) for just $11.95. We'll SAVE 54% off the cover price! If we choose not to subscribe, we'll return the bill marked "cancel", and owe nothing. The FREE issue is ours to keep.

_____
Name   (please print)

_____
Address

_____
City/State/Zip

_____
(Optional) gender of child/children (boy/girl)   Birthdate(s)

FamilyFun's newsstand price is $25.90 a year. In Canada, add $10 (U.S. funds) for postage and GST. Other foreign orders, add $20 (U.S. funds). First issue mails within 6-8 weeks. Offer valid through June 30, 2000. © Disney

FamilyFun HOLIDAYS
SPECIAL ISSUE
Best Toys
3rd Annual T.O.Y. Awards
46-Page Guide
Kids' Crafts
Cards, Gifts & Ornaments
Parties

FamilyFun Special Issue
CRAFTS
After-School Play!
Finger puppets, model boats, and a homemade birdhouse
26 WACKY CUPCAKES
10 NEW WAYS TO USE CRAYONS
Easy Musical...

Includes
TWO SPECIAL ISSUES
at no extra cost!

L7MW

FamilyFun

100% activities. 100% fun.

From **Disney**

"Your magazine is absolutely fantastic! It has everything I have been looking for in a magazine and have never been able to find."

— Peggy Bertsch,
Sandusky, Ohio

"Fresh ideas for getting involved with my kids — isn't that what parenting is all about? Thank you, thank you, thank you."

— Cathy Zirkelbach,
Denver, Colorado

"This is the best magazine for families I have ever seen. I will keep my issues forever."

— Carol A. Green,
Lee's Summit, Missouri

"I have read FamilyFun front to back twice and have shared articles with almost everyone I know. Our family has tried recipes and activities — and we haven't had a flop yet! I only wish we had discovered you sooner."

— Mary Balcom,
Rochester Hills,
Michigan

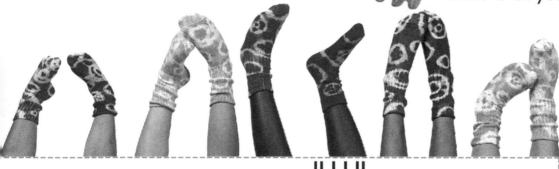

FREE ISSUE!

FamilyFun
Great Island Towns!
Beach Vacations Families Love
HOST A COWBOY COOKOUT
You Can Hike with Kids
18 Top Family Dogs
Crafts for Beachcombers!

Yours free!

See why families everywhere are having so much fun with FamilyFun! Send for your FREE ISSUE today. If card is missing, write to FamilyFun Magazine, PO Box 37031, Boone, IA 50037-2031.